Tarantula Toes

Beverly Lewis

Beverly Lewis Books for Young Readers

PICTURE BOOKS

Annika's Secret Wish
Cows in the House
Just Like Mama

THE CUL-DE-SAC KIDS

The Double Dabble Surprise
The Chicken Pox Panic
The Crazy Christmas Angel Mystery
No Grown-ups Allowed
Frog Power
The Mystery of Case D. Luc
The Stinky Sneakers Mystery
Pickle Pizza
Mailbox Mania
The Mudhole Mystery
Fiddlesticks
The Crabby Cat Caper
Tarantula Toes
Green Gravy
Backyard Bandit Mystery
Tree House Trouble
The Creepy Sleep-Over
The Great TV Turn-Off
Piggy Party
The Granny Game
Mystery Mutt
Big Bad Beans
The Upside-Down Day
The Midnight Mystery

Katie and Jake and the Haircut Mistake

THE CUL-DE-SAC KIDS

Tarantula Toes

Beverly Lewis

BETHANY HOUSE PUBLISHERS
MINNEAPOLIS, MINNESOTA 55438

Tarantula Toes
Copyright © 1997
Beverly Lewis

Cover illustration by Paul Turnbaugh
Text illustrations by Janet Huntington

Published by Bethany House Publishers
11400 Hampshire Avenue South
Bloomington, Minnesota 55438

Bethany House Publishers is a division of
Baker Publishing Group, Grand Rapids, Michigan.

Printed in the United States of America

Library of Congress Cataloging-in-Publication Data

Lewis, Beverly, 1949–
    Tarantula toes / by Beverly Lewis
       p.   cm. — (the cul-de-sac kids)
    Summary: Jason cannot wait to get his new pet tarantula, but the other members of the Cul-de-sac Kids don't share his excitement.
    ISBN 1-55661-984-7 (pbk.)
    [1. Tarantulas—Fiction. 2. Friendship—Fiction.]
I. Title. II. Title. III. Series: Lewis, Beverly, 1949–
Cul-de-sac kids.
PZ7.L58464Tar   1997
[Fic]—dc21   97–21031
                                     CIP
                                       AC

To
three of my young fans,
all in one family!

Chris, Collin, and Linsi Stoddard.

THE CUL-DE-SAC KIDS

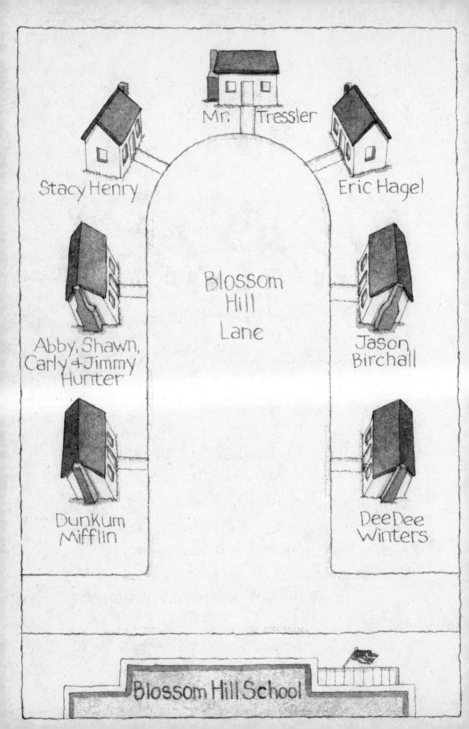

ONE

Jason Birchall zipped through his homework.

I have to tell someone my secret! he thought.

He didn't bother to check his spelling. He didn't even read over his work.

Jason was in such a big hurry. He slapped his name on the paper and pushed his homework into a folder.

Then he dashed outside.

It was still light, so he jumped on his bike.

His friends, Dunkum and Eric, were

already out riding. They zoomed up Blossom Hill Lane when they saw him. "Hey, Jason!" they called. "Wanna ride?"

"You bet!" Jason said.

"Did you finish your homework already?" Dunkum asked. He was always talking school stuff.

"Ya-hoo! It's done," Jason hollered. "But let's not talk about that."

He glanced around.

Was it safe?

He made his voice sound mysterious. "Listen up, guys."

Eric stared at Jason. "Why are you talking like that?" Eric said.

"Because," said Jason.

"Because why?" Dunkum asked.

"Because I've got a secret," Jason said.

"So tell us," Eric said. "I'm sure you're dying to."

Jason smiled. His friends knew him well. "OK, I'll tell you. But you have to promise not to say one word to the girls."

Dunkum's face lit up. "You can trust us. You know that."

Eric agreed. "We promise."

Jason looked over his shoulder. "Are we really alone?"

Dunkum nodded. "It's just us guys."

"Let's not take any chances," Jason said. He motioned to Eric and Dunkum. And the three of them headed up the driveway. When they reached the garage door, Jason whispered, "I'm starting up a zoo."

"*That's* your secret?" Dunkum said.

"Shh!" Jason peered around, checking for other Cul-de-sac Kids. "It's top secret."

"Are we talking a real zoo?" Eric asked.

Jason leaned a little closer. "You heard right. June is Zoo Month, so I'm starting a REAL zoo in my room."

Eric scratched his head. "Does your mom know about this?"

"My parents think it'll be an adventure."

"You mean like a learning experience?" Dunkum said with a frown.

"That's exactly right." Jason reached into his pocket. He unfolded a page out of the newspaper.

Eric leaned on his bike for a closer look. "Whatcha got?"

"Check out my super-secret," Jason said. He pointed to a picture of a big, hairy spider. "I'm gonna buy *this* tomorrow."

Eric did a gulp. "Is . . . is that what I think it is?"

"It's a tarantula, all right," Jason said proudly.

"Hey, let me see." Dunkum grabbed the paper. "Whoa, Willie Millie! I can almost see Abby Hunter's hair sticking straight up!"

Abby was the president of the Cul-de-sac Kids. Nine kids on one block. A really cool club.

Jason started jumping around. "Stacy Henry will freak out, too. So will Dee Dee and Carly!" he chanted.

"Wow, what a scary spider!" Eric said. "Are you buying him just to scare the girls?"

"Shh! How can you say that?" Jason said. But he didn't stop grinning or hopping. He felt good all over. "It's a pink-toed tarantula. And tomorrow he's all mine!"

"I don't know about this," Dunkum said. He studied the picture a little longer. "A tarantula might not be such a good idea."

Jason pushed up his glasses. "What do you mean?"

"They eat frogs, right?" asked Dunkum.

Jason started to laugh. "Oh, I get it! You're thinking about Croaker. But you shouldn't be. My new pet will NOT be eating frogs."

14

Jason knew exactly what to feed Pinktoes. His spider book told all about tarantulas. Everything he needed to know. There was even a chapter on how to handle spiders.

"Crickets and earthworms are Pinktoe's favorite snacks," Jason spoke up.

"Well, good luck finding insects like that around here," Dunkum said. He handed the newspaper back.

Jason looked at Dunkum. His friend was probably right. Crickets needed plenty of oxygen. The air was thin in this part of Colorado.

"Don't worry," Jason said. "I'll take good care of Pinktoes. You'll see. I might even let him crawl on me."

Dunkum's eyes were big and black now. Really black. "What about fangs?" he asked. "Don't tarantulas bite?"

"*I'm* not afraid," Jason bragged.

Eric looked a little pale.

Dunkum looked worried.

15

"I'll have Pinktoes by tomorrow," Jason said. "Then you'll see how brave I am."

"Tomorrow? That soon?" Eric said.

Before Jason could answer, Eric hopped on his bike and rode away.

Dunkum did, too.

Jason wasn't surprised. Some kids were just 'fraidy cats. But not him. He was going to be brave. He was going to be the bravest kid in the world.

Besides, no one else had a zoo in their bedroom.

No one else had a pink-toed tarantula. All the way from South America.

Not one single Cul-de-sac Kid did. Not one!

I'll be the only tarantula keeper around, he thought.

He could hardly wait.

TWO

At last, it was Saturday.

Tarantula time!

Jason awoke early, even before his parents.

Rolling over, he found the newspaper ad. Right where he'd left it—under his pillow!

He burst out laughing. Dunkum and Eric would shake with fear. They'd shiver and shake if they knew. He was sure they would.

Whoever slept on a picture of spiders? Kids with courage. That's who!

Just then his father called to him. "What's so funny over there?"

His dad was up. Yes!

Jason rushed into the hallway. He stood at his parents' bedroom door. "Ready for a visit to the pet store?" he asked.

His mother made funny little noises. She sounded half asleep.

The door opened.

Mr. Birchall was wearing a bathrobe. "You're up too early, son," he said.

Jason pushed his glasses up. "Because I can't wait. Let's go get my spider!"

His father smiled and headed for the kitchen.

Jason was right on his heels. "C'mon, let's go NOW!"

"Are you really sure about this spider purchase?" Dad asked. "Have you thought it through?"

Jason couldn't believe his ears.

"Of course I'm sure," he said. "The

tank's all set up. Everything's ready."

"And you followed all the directions?"

Jason nodded. "I followed everything exactly right."

Dad smiled. "And you'll be very careful if you decide to handle your new pet?"

"*If* I do? I KNOW I will!"

His father put a firm hand on Jason's shoulder. "You must be gentle, son. Tarantulas are delicate pets."

"I'll be the best spider keeper ever," Jason promised. "You'll see."

★ ★ ★

Jason got dressed for the day. In a hurry. He heard his dad humming in the shower.

Bacon-and-egg smells floated from the kitchen.

"Today's tarantula day," he told his mother.

"What a brave one you are," she said. "I don't know how you even look at those

19

spiders. And to think one of those hairy things is coming to live in my house."

"Pinktoes will live in *my* bedroom," Jason reminded her. "He'll stay in his tank . . . most of the time."

Mrs. Birchall's hand flew to her throat. "Most of the time? Don't you mean *all* of the time?"

"Oh, not when I'm showing him off," Jason explained. "Sometimes he'll be on display."

His mother's eyebrows arched. "Oh?"

"There's nothing to worry about. Nothing at all."

"I hope not." She wiped her forehead. "I really do."

At breakfast, Jason and his parents talked even more. All about the spider.

"He needs cork bark to climb on," Jason said.

"We'll buy some today," Dad said. "Crickets too."

"I'll dig for earthworms after lunch,"

20

Jason suggested. "A tasty treat for a tarantula."

"Good thinking," Mother said. She wrinkled up her nose. The subject of worms was a no-no at the table.

"Uh . . . sorry, Mom," Jason said.

"It would be much better if we talk *after* we eat," she said.

A wink came from Jason's father.

And Jason understood.

But gross stuff didn't bother him. Not one bit. Worms or crickets, spiders and frogs were just fine.

Any old time!

THREE

The ride downtown took forever.

Rush. Faster. Hurry . . . hurry, thought Jason.

Even the light stayed red too long.

Jitter, jitter. Jump, jerk. Jason couldn't sit still.

"Excited?" asked his dad.

"Pinktoes comes home today!" Jason said.

Then he spied the pet shop sign.

His father parked the car. "Have you told your friends yet?" he asked.

"I told only two."

"Boys?" His father was grinning.

"I told Dunkum and Eric. They promised not to tell it around," Jason explained.

"So it's a secret?"

"A super-spider super-secret!" Jason said. He leaped out of the car and raced to the pet store.

Inside, a large glass tank was waiting. A tiny tan spider was perched in the corner.

Pinktoes was nowhere to be seen.

"Where's my spider?" Jason wailed.

The clerk hurried over. "May I help you?"

"Where's Pinktoes?"

"Wait one moment," said the clerk.

Jason took off his glasses and twirled them on his finger. He jittered and jived.

"Someone bought my spider," he fussed. "Bought him out from under my nose!"

His father shook his head. "Don't

worry, son. Here comes the store owner."

A tall man smiled at them. "We're getting more pink-toed tarantulas in on Monday."

"*Two* more days? That's way too long," Jason said.

"Sorry about the wait," the man said. "I'll be happy to put your name on one."

"*My* name?" Jason looked at his dad.

"He means he'll save one for you," his father explained.

"Oh . . . sure, that would be great!" Jason burst out.

But he didn't feel great inside.

Nope.

Dunkum and Eric would never believe this. They'd think he was fooling about getting a super-spider. They'd say he was making it all up.

"We'll be back on Monday," Jason's father said.

"Right after school," added Jason. "And not a minute later!"

His father nodded.
The pet store owner waved.
And Jason scuffed his feet to the car.

★ ★ ★

The ride home went too fast.
All green lights.
Phooey.
Jason scooted down in the front seat.
He didn't want Dunkum and Eric to see
him. Not without Pinktoes.
How will I tell them? he thought.
Then he had an idea. He'd say that
Pinktoes was crawling home. He'd say
that the tarantula was last seen headed
this way. A big, black tarantula was on
the loose. Headed for Blossom Hill Lane!
That's what Jason decided.
It was a whoppin' big lie.
But Dunkum and Eric would be scared
silly.

FOUR

The car was hardly in the driveway.
Here came Dunkum and Eric, running.

Rats! thought Jason.

Dunkum called to him from behind a tree. "Where's your big, mean spider?" he said.

Jason glanced over at his dad. He didn't want him to hear what he was going to say.

"Hello, boys," his dad said, waving at Dunkum and Eric. Then he went inside the house.

Jason got out of the car. He stood tall.

Now he could tell his made-up story.

"I thought you were buying a hairy monster," Dunkum said. "Where is it?"

The boys stayed close to the tree.

"And *I* thought you were too scared to see it," Jason replied.

"Well, we're not," Eric said. "We're braver than you think."

Jason lowered his voice. "Well, if you really wanna know, he's on the loose. And coming this way!"

Eric looked around. "I don't see anything."

"You just wait," Jason said. But he felt funny inside.

Dunkum scratched his head. He inched close. "You mean your pet spider is crawling here? To Blossom Hill Lane?"

It sounded very fishy. Foolish too.

Jason almost laughed at his own words. But he pulled himself together. "You heard me," he said. "Pinktoes is on the prowl. He's coming. You better watch out!"

Eric was still staring at the ground, looking for super-spiders. "Better break your secret and warn the girls, then," Eric said. "They won't wanna see a scary spider around here."

"No!" Jason shouted. "Don't tell them. We have to keep it a secret."

"How come?" Dunkum said. He was still frowning.

He doesn't believe me, thought Jason. *He knows I'm lying.*

"So . . . what's the expected time of arrival?" asked Dunkum. "For your tarantula, I mean."

"Oh, I don't know," Jason spoke up. "It might take him till Monday."

It was sort of true. But not really.

Eric stared at him. "Can spiders smell their way? Like dogs and cats do?"

Jason swallowed hard.

Rats.

What could he say? More lies?

"Uh, I don't know for sure," he mumbled. "Maybe they can. But I think I hear my mother calling."

"I don't hear anything," Eric said. He looked at Dunkum.

"Me neither," Dunkum said.

Both boys gave Jason a weird look.

"Go ahead and find your mother," Dunkum said. His face had a big grin. "Eric and I will be on the lookout for your tarantula."

"Don't step on him," Jason warned. "He's part of my zoo."

Dunkum Mitchell, whose real name was Edward, laughed out loud. He laughed all the way down the cul-de-sac.

"Double rats!" Jason said to himself.

★ ★ ★

Jason could hardly eat lunch.

His hamburger stuck in his throat.

"What's wrong, dear?" his mother asked.

"I'm not hungry," he replied.

"Are you sick?" she asked.

Sick of lying, he thought. But he didn't say that.

He didn't know what to do. Dunkum and Eric would never believe him now. Not even if he tried to tell the truth.

The whole truth.

He'd just have to wait. Two more days.

By Monday everyone would know about Pinktoes. Especially Dunkum and Eric. Then they could see for themselves.

But Jason was worried.

What if the spider shipment didn't come? What would he tell his friends? Another made-up story?

He carried his plate to the sink.

"Sorry about your spider," his mother said.

His father spoke up. "It's supposed to arrive on Monday."

Jason shrugged.

Supposed to, he thought.

He felt even worse.

33

FIVE

On Monday, math class took forever.

Yuck times two, thought Jason.

Science lasted too long. So did morning and afternoon recess.

Double phooey.

Jason didn't say much to Dunkum or Eric. And they didn't ask about Pinktoes.

I hope they're keeping my secret, Jason thought.

But he knew better. They didn't believe him.

Not one bit.

★ ★ ★

After school, Jason waited for his father.

Time to go to the pet store. Again!

This time, Jason didn't go near the glassed-in tank.

He was a jittery worry-bug. He crossed his fingers behind his back.

The clerk came right over. "Jason Birchall, right? We have a pink-toed tarantula with your name on it."

Jason couldn't help it. He smiled. "Cool stuff," he said.

The spider shipment had come!

Now Dunkum and Eric could freak out. They could be 'fraidy cats. But best of all, they'd believe him.

Jason peeked at the glass tank. He whispered, "How's it going, Pinktoes?"

The spider was still as the moon.

Was he breathing?

Nothing moved. Not even his fangs.

"Today you're gonna be a Cul-de-Sac Kid's pet. *My* pet," Jason explained.

36

The black spider started to move. His long legs crawled toward the glass. He came up to Jason's face, on the other side of the glass.

"Excuse me, young man," the clerk said.

Jason stepped back.

The man removed the top on the tank.

Jason pointed to the black tarantula. "I want that one." The spider's long legs had pinkish spots on the tips.

"He's beautiful," said the clerk. "A very good choice. I hope you've read up on these furry fellows."

"Oh yes," Jason replied. "I know all about them."

"Then you know how to pick them up?" the man asked.

Jason nodded. "With my fingers away from its fangs."

"Very good." Then the man showed how to handle the spider.

"That's how my spider book said to do

it," said Jason, watching.

"OK," said the clerk. "You're all set."

Ya-hoo!

Jason felt like a billion bucks. But he only had twenty-five. Plenty to buy his new pet.

His father spoke up. "Jason knows a lot about *frogs*, too."

"Oh?" the man said. "Do you own a frog?"

"Yes, but Croaker and Pinktoes won't be tank mates," Jason was quick to say. "Besides, Pinktoes doesn't eat frogs."

The clerk's eyelids blinked. "You're one hundred percent correct."

"I *have* to be," Jason said. "It's Zoo Month. And I'm starting my very own zoo."

"A zoo?"

"A zoo in my room." Jason grinned.

"An excellent place for your Pinktoes," said the clerk. "Now, that'll be nineteen dollars."

Flash! Out came Jason's wallet. He'd saved up for a long time.

"Just one spider today?" asked the man.

"One for now," Jason said. "Maybe more later."

"We'll see about that," his father said. "We'll see what kind of zoo keeper you are."

Jason smiled a big smile. The best part of the day had finally come.

Pinktoes was going home.

Hoo-ray!

SIX

After supper, Jason went to Dunkum's house.

"There's a super-spider in the cul-de-sac," he said.

"Yeah, right," Dunkum's eyes narrowed.

"I'm *not* kidding," Jason said. "Come over and see for yourself."

Dunkum rolled his eyes. "He didn't *really* crawl all the way from the pet store. Did he?"

Jason shook his head. "I should've told you the truth before. I'm sorry."

"Why'd you lie?"

Jason shrugged his shoulders. "I thought you'd laugh at me. I thought—"

"Forget it," Dunkum said. "Just don't do it again. Deal?"

"Double deal." Jason started to feel better inside. "When do you wanna see Pinktoes?" he asked.

"Maybe after school," Dunkum said, but he looked like he didn't believe Jason.

"OK, see you then." Jason ran next door to Abby Hunter's house.

He invited her and Carly, her little sister, over. And their adopted Korean brothers, Shawn and Jimmy.

"Yikes, I don't know," Abby said. "Sounds creepy. Do you *really* have a tarantula?"

Jason grinned. "Sure do! And Pinktoes will stay in his tank. Don't worry."

Carly and Jimmy came to the door.

"Wanna go see Jason's tarantula?"

Abby asked them. "He says it's from South America."

"Right," Jimmy said. "Spider no get here from there." He was still learning to speak English.

Carly took two steps back. "A tarantula? Nobody has pets like *that*!" Her eyes were wide and round.

Jason stood tall. "He looks very scary. I thought I should warn you."

"Well, Carly and I probably won't come then," Abby said.

"Jimmy not think there is big spider!" shouted Jimmy. "No way."

Jason scratched his head. "Well, there is. Better come tomorrow and see for yourself."

Next, he went to Stacy Henry's house.

"No, thanks," she said. "I HATE spiders!"

"Too bad for you," he said.

Jason crossed the street.

Eric Hagel would be dying to see

43

Pinktoes. Jason was sure of it. Eric would be scared silly, but he'd come anyway.

Jason was right about his friend.

"Promise to leave your spider in the tank?" Eric said. "If you *really* own a Pinktoes."

"I really do," Jason said. "And I'll keep him in the tank."

Next he headed for Dee Dee Winter's house.

She was playing outside with her crabby cat, Mister Whiskers.

"Wanna come see my tarantula?" Jason asked.

"EEEEE-EEW!" Dee Dee screamed. "Get away from me, Jason Birchall! Don't make up lies!"

"Sorry I stopped by," Jason muttered.

He pulled himself together and marched home.

SEVEN

It was Tuesday.

Miss Hershey was writing on the board. Her back was to the class.

Perfect!

Jason glanced at Abby Hunter.

When she looked at him, he made his fingers wiggle and crawl. Just like a spider. A big one.

Abby shook her head and frowned at him.

Erase boards, Miss Hershey wrote. *Stacy Henry.*

Stacy grinned, probably because erasing boards was her favorite job.

"Lucky Stacy," someone whispered.

Jason stared at Stacy. Then he made his spider-y hand.

Stacy's eyebrows floated up. She looked the other way.

Miss Hershey wrote on the board: *Hamster helper—Jason Birchall.*

Jason sat tall. *Ya-hoo!*

Feeding the hamster was the best job. The coolest for a zoo keeper. A zoo-in-his-room keeper!

The class said the pledge.

"I pledge allegiance to the flag," Jason began. But he was thinking about his tarantula.

He couldn't stop thinking about Pinktoes. He thought so hard, he missed six spelling words. He thought so long, he forgot to feed the hamster.

"What is wrong today?" Shawn Hunter asked at recess.

"Nothing," Jason said. "Are you

coming to my house after school?"

"To see fake spider?"

"Didn't Abby tell you?" Jason asked.

"Abby not tell me. Jimmy, little brother, tell about pretend spider." Shawn's eyes nearly closed shut.

"So . . . are you coming?" asked Jason.

"I not believe you," Shawn said.

Jason shrugged. Nobody did.

He was the coolest, bravest tarantula owner around. And no one believed him!

Then they ran to the soccer field.

★　★　★

After school, Jason stood on his front porch.

He wondered if maybe, just maybe, someone would show up. The sun was in his eyes. So he sat on the step.

What's wrong with me? he thought. *Why don't my friends believe me?*

Across the street, Carly and Dee Dee were cutting out paper dolls.

47

Abby and Stacy were walking their dogs.

The boys were nowhere to be seen.

Jason waited and waited. He went inside to check the clock.

Next, he went to his room.

Everything was set.

Croaker seemed well-behaved. He sat quietly in his glass home on the dresser. He blinked his eyes at Jason.

Pinktoes was in his tank on the bookcase. He flicked his fangs.

The zoo-room was absolutely perfect.

Jason tiptoed to Pinktoe's tank. "I think everyone's a 'fraidy cat," he said. "Everyone on Blossom Hill Lane!"

Pinktoes looked like he was snoozing. He didn't budge a single black hair. He was probably dreaming about his next cricket.

Jason went to the living room. He sat on the sofa.

He stayed there till supper.

But no one showed up. Not a single brave kid.

"It's very quiet around here," his mother said.

Jason got up and helped set the table.

"I was sorta expecting company," he said. "But no one came."

"That's strange," she said. "Don't the Cul-de-Sac Kids stick together?"

"What?" Jason said.

His mother repeated the familiar words.

That's it, Jason thought. *They're sticking together! They think I'm lying . . . again.*

He felt foolish. And very upset.

Just then an idea hit him.

"I'll show them I'm not lying," he whispered to himself. "I'll take Pinktoes' picture!"

He was going to prove himself.

The Cul-de-sac Kids would have to believe him now.

Then he had another idea.

It was a better-than-good idea.

He would have a spider show. He'd invite all the kids. They could see the picture, then come to his amazing show. *Ya-hoo!*

EIGHT

After supper, Jason took a bunch of pictures. He used his dad's instant camera. Then he made invitations. Eight in all. One for every Cul-de-sac Kid. Not counting himself.

He drew a big, black spider on the front, then he wrote the message.

Jason licked each envelope shut.

He thought of all the money he would make.

What a super-cool idea.

Eight kids times seventy-five cents. Six whole bucks!

COme see
Jason BIrChall,
TaraTula Tamer!!!
Featuring a SouthAmerican
Super Spider, Pink Toes!!
(fierce fangs, Venom, and ALL!!!)
When? Thursday after school
Where? Jason's front yard
How much? 75 Cents per Kid

Six dollars would buy a lot of crickets. If only he could get the kids to come.

He could hear Dunkum bouncing his basketball. That was the first house. He stuck the invitation and the instant picture of Pinktoes on the front door.

Dunkum glanced his way. "Whatcha got?"

"Something for you." Jason forced a smile.

"Oh . . . thanks," Dunkum said. But he was frowning again.

"You didn't show up today," Jason said.

Dunkum shot a basket. "I know."

"Well, I thought we had a deal. You know, about not lying?" Jason said.

"I never promised to come."

"Did too," Jason said.

Dunkum shook his head. "I said 'maybe.' "

Jason shook his head. He wasn't going to push for answers. He'd let the invitation and the picture do their jobs.

53

"Well . . . see ya," Jason said. And he left.

At Abby's house, he stuffed four invitations in the screen door. One for each Hunter kid.

Then he went around the block and delivered the rest.

He almost stopped to visit Mr. Tressler. He was the old man at the end of the cul-de-sac.

But Jason was too busy. He had some practicing to do. Lots of it.

The Brave Tarantula Tamer had a cool super-spider. But no amazing act to go with it.

So he hurried home.

First things first. He needed a pair of thin rubber gloves. Something to protect his hands.

He borrowed his mother's kitchen gloves. They were too big. Better than nothing.

Jason dashed to his bedroom. "OK,

Pinktoes, it's you and me," he said.

Gently, he took off the lid and reached inside.

Very slowly, the tarantula crawled onto his gloved hand.

"Nice and easy," he whispered.

He had a jumpy stomach. But he had to be brave.

Pinktoes mustn't sense his fear. Not now. Not for their first time together.

"Here you go," he said softly.

Jason put his left hand next to his right. He held them close together. That way Pinktoes wouldn't fall.

He must NOT fall, because his body was very delicate. Falling could be a deadly thing.

Pinktoes went from one hand to the other.

It tickled. Jason got goose pimples on his goose bumps.

"Cool stuff," he said, but not too loudly. He didn't want to scare his new zoo friend.

"Can you do it again?" he said.

Jason moved his hand back. He held his breath.

The tarantula kept going.

"Good for you," Jason said.

He didn't want to tire Pinktoes out. So he put him back in the glass tank.

"We'll practice again tomorrow. OK?"

Pinktoes did not reply. Anyone knows tarantulas don't talk.

Still, Jason waited. He watched his spider climb the cork bark. "We're having a show in two days," whispered Jason.

Could he pull it off?

Jason tried not to worry. He looked out his bedroom window.

The Hunter kids—Abby, Carly, Shawn, and Jimmy—sat on their front steps. They were looking at his invitations. And the pictures.

Will they come? he wondered.

Silently, he closed the curtains.

He crossed his fingers and hoped so.

NINE

The next morning, Jason got up before the sun.

He pulled on his mother's kitchen gloves. Time to practice his spider act.

Today he was more sure of himself. Much more.

And things went very well.

Jason decided he was braver now. He would practice without the gloves after breakfast.

His mother wasn't told about it. Nope.

This was top secret.

Jason made his hands flat and firm.

Pinktoes crawled over them.

It tickled just a little. But Jason felt comfortable with his pet.

No gloves. And no bites.

Perfect.

"We'll practice again right after school," he said.

And off he went to school, feeling braver than ever.

★ ★ ★

During recess, he had an idea. It was kinda crazy.

He watched Jimmy Hunter playing in the sand pit. Jimmy was barefoot.

That's when the idea hit.

Could Pinktoes walk over my bare toes? Jason thought.

He laughed out loud and couldn't wait to find out.

"What's so funny?" a small voice said.

Jason spun around.

It was Dee Dee Winters.

"Oh, hi," he said.

"Why are you laughing?" she asked. "I don't see anything funny."

"Oh, it's nothing," Jason said.

Dee Dee made her face twist up. "Well, I don't know about that, Jason Birchall. Laughing over nothing is pretty weird."

He stood as tall as he could. "Oh, you'll see."

"See what?"

"You'll see what's so funny if you come to my show. If you're *brave* enough."

"Come to a silly spider show? Why would I wanna do that?" Dee Dee giggled.

Jason hated it when she giggled. But he kept smiling. "Because it's gonna be amazing. I'm gonna handle my tarantula with *bare hands*!" he replied. "That's why you should come."

"Really?" Her eyes were bright now.

"Oh, it's gonna be so thrilling. Creepy, crawly stuff. Fangs and venom—you

know, spider stuff. Better come and see."
Jason grinned.

Surely this would get her attention.

The other Cul-de-sac Kids would probably hear about it, too.

Dee Dee was a little girl with a big
mouth. She would spread the word.

Jason was counting on it.

TEN

Thursday afternoon came quickly.

All the Cul-de-sac Kids were gathered in Jason's front yard.

He couldn't believe his eyes.

Good work, Dee Dee, he thought. Her blabby mouth had worked wonders.

"This is super great," he told Pinktoes. "They've come for the show."

He carried the glass tank out to the front porch. Carefully, he set it down.

Then he turned to greet his friends. "Welcome to the most amazing spider show on earth!"

He wished he had a trio of trumpets. He could hear them in his head. *Tah-dah-dah-DAH!*

"Everyone sit on the grass," he said. "Make yourselves comfortable."

He was having a double dabble good time. That's what Abby always liked to say.

Dee Dee and Carly seemed nervous, though. Abby would call them jitterboxes for sure. Which was the truth.

Abby and her best friend, Stacy Henry, were standing nearby. Eyes wide.

Dunkum and Eric sat crosslegged in the grass. Shawn and Jimmy Hunter seemed excited. A little bit.

First things first.

Jason passed his baseball cap around. *Chinkle . . . chink.* The kids dropped their money inside.

Jason was laughing under his breath. His trick was working. They'd all come to see his daring show. A super-spider show.

But there was something his friends didn't know. The best spider secret known to man. It was the BIG secret about the spider's fangs!

He couldn't wait to fool his friends.

"I will now pick up the tarantula," Jason announced. "Quiet, please. Pinktoes will perform best if it's quiet."

Dee Dee and Carly giggled. But they seemed edgy.

Whispers rippled through the group. Someone said something about the fangs. And the venom.

It was perfect. The kids were really scared.

"Shh!" Jason said. "I must have it quiet."

He waited for the group to settle down.

Finally, no one spoke.

He picked up his tarantula. Very carefully he sat down in the grass.

Slowly, he passed his gloved hands back and forth.

Carly was hiding her eyes. Dee Dee was peeking.

Abby and Stacy looked absolutely frightened.

But the boys looked brave. Dunkum and Eric watched without blinking. Shawn and Jimmy smiled brave smiles.

Jason was glad. His friends were enjoying the show.

And he was tricking them. Again.

He put his spider in the glass tank. He removed the gloves. Next, he reached back in and picked up the tarantula again.

The sound of *Ooh*s could be heard. From the girls, mostly.

Dunkum whispered, "Willie Millie!"

"Now I will let Pinktoes crawl on my bare hands," Jason said. "Remember, he has fangs!"

Dee Dee and Carly squeaked a little.

But not another sound was heard.

Jason held his tarantula correctly. Far

away from the fangs.

He sat on the grass again. Then he crossed his legs. One bare foot stuck high in the air.

Without a sound, he set the tarantula on his toes.

Jason grinned and put his hands behind his head.

"Tah-dah!" he said. "Just call me Mister Tarantula Toes!"

Quickly, he reached to free his pet from the high perch.

But before he could, Pinktoes jumped into the air.

Plop!

The tarantula landed on Jason's head.

"Eeee-eew!" the girls screamed.

Jason felt a stab of pain in his forehead.

"Ouch!" he hollered. "The fangs!"

ELEVEN

"Jason, Jason, are you all right?" Abby said.

The Cul-de-sac Kids gathered around.

"Is he gonna die?" Carly asked.

"Lie still," Jason's mother said to him. She looked at Jason's friends. "Why do you think he might die?" she asked.

Jason spoke up. He felt terrible, but not from the spider bite. "People don't die from spider venom," he mumbled.

Eric frowned. "But you said—"

"I tricked you on purpose," Jason said. "I didn't tell the truth about Pinktoes."

69

His mother finished treating the wound.

Soon Jason sat up and looked at each kid. "I wanted to fool you, to get back at all of you for not believing me."

"Well, you did a good job of it," Stacy said.

"He sure did!" Dee Dee said.

Jason felt the tiny lump on his forehead. "I shouldn't have made you think Pinktoes was a monster. With poison in his fangs."

"Well, he *is* scary-looking," Stacy said.

"I think he's beautiful," said Jason.

"Not to me," Abby said.

Jason began to explain. "Tarantulas are gentle pets. Their bites are milder than a beesting."

"What about that nasty bump on your head?" Dee Dee pointed to the swelling. "That doesn't look so good."

"It'll go away," Jason's mother said.

She helped him up. "It's nothing to worry about."

"For sure?" Carly asked.

Jason smiled and nodded. His friends cared about him. They really did.

He wanted to be a better friend. Starting right now.

"Pinktoes was terrified," Jason said. "That's the only reason he bit me. Tarantulas don't bite unless they're frightened. Or feel in danger. I never should've put him up so high."

The kids peeked inside the glass tank. They wanted to see the jumping spider up close. And his giant web.

All except Dee Dee and Carly. They didn't want to look.

Dunkum and Eric inched closer to the tank. "Can we feed Pinktoes sometime?"

"Sure," Jason said. "Wanna help me dig for his supper?"

"When?" said Shawn Hunter.

"Right now," answered Jason.

Shawn rubbed his hands together. His dark eyes twinkled.

"Remember *The Mudhole Mystery?*" said Jason.

"Sure do!" Dunkum said. "Ooey, gooey worms are fun."

"Worms are NOT fun. Worms are supposed to be spider snacks," someone said.

Jason and the boys turned around.

It was Abby Hunter. She was hiding something behind her.

"Whatcha got?" Jason asked. He tried to peek around her.

Abby stepped back. "I'll show you if you make a promise," she said.

Jason shrugged. "What kind of promise?"

"No more lies?" she said.

Dunkum and Eric were laughing.

But Abby wasn't. "Well?" she said.

Jason pinched up his face. Being pushed into a corner was no fun. Especially by a girl.

"I'm waiting," she said.

Dunkum was holding his sides. He was laughing too hard.

"The club president has spoken," Eric said.

Jason teased, "But is she brave?"

Abby held out a jar of wiggly worms. "Here's proof."

"Hey, cool," said Jason. "Thanks!"

Abby put her hands on her hips. "*Now* do you promise?"

"OK, OK," Jason said. "I promise. And I mean it."

She smiled. "You're a double dabble mischief," Abby said. "But a good friend."

"You can say that again," Dunkum said.

Shawn Hunter spoke up. He said it again. "Jason is double dabble good friend. He very good friend."

It came out like *velly* good.

But Jason didn't mind. Not one bit.

THE CUL-DE-SAC KIDS SERIES
Don't miss #14!

GREEN GRAVY

Carly Hunter is chosen "Student of the Week" two days before St. Patrick's Day. Her classmates must wear green, because she's Irish. And Carly wants everyone to eat only green foods, too, during lunch.

But Jimmy, her adopted Korean brother, doesn't want to join the silly custom. He thinks foods that are green are yucky.

Who will win in this brother-sister tug-of-war?

ABOUT THE AUTHOR

Beverly Lewis remembers picking worms off her father's strawberry plants when she was a kid. But spiders? Nope!

While researching tarantula facts for this book, Beverly visited two pet stores and the public library. "I felt as jumpy as Jason Birchall," she admits. "Back at my desk, I covered up the creepy-crawly pictures. I didn't want to see even *one* hairy spider out of the corner of my eye!"

The idea to write this book came from her son. He thought it was time for a Cul-de-sac Kids book mostly for boys. "But brave girls are welcome!" says the author.

If you like humor and mystery mixed together, look for all the Cul-de-sac Kids books. Don't be too surprised by what you may see on the cover!

Also by Beverly Lewis

The Beverly Lewis Amish Heritage Cookbook

GIRLS ONLY (GO!)
Youth Fiction

Dreams on Ice	*Follow the Dream*
Only the Best	*Better Than Best*
A Perfect Match	*Photo Perfect*
Reach for the Stars	*Star Status*

SUMMERHILL SECRETS
Youth Fiction

Whispers Down the Lane	*House of Secrets*
Secret in the Willows	*Echoes in the Wind*
Catch a Falling Star	*Hide Behind the Moon*
Night of the Fireflies	*Windows on the Hill*
A Cry in the Dark	*Shadows Beyond the Gate*

HOLLY'S HEART
Youth Fiction

Best Friend, Worst Enemy	*Straight-A Teacher*
Secret Summer Dreams	*No Guys Pact*
Sealed With a Kiss	*Little White Lies*
The Trouble With Weddings	*Freshman Frenzy*
California Crazy	*Mystery Letters*
Second-Best Friend	*Eight Is Enough*
Good-Bye, Dressel Hills	*It's a Girl Thing*

ABRAM'S DAUGHTERS
Adult Fiction

The Covenant • *The Betrayal* • *The Sacrifice*
The Prodigal • *The Revelation*

ANNIE'S PEOPLE
Adult Fiction

The Preacher's Daughter • *The Englisher*

THE HERITAGE OF LANCASTER COUNTY
Adult Fiction

The Shunning • *The Confession* • *The Reckoning*

OTHER ADULT FICTION

The Postcard • *The Crossroad*
The Redemption of Sarah Cain
October Song • *Sanctuary** • *The Sunroom*

www.BeverlyLewis.com

*with David Lewis

From Bethany House Publishers

Series for Beginning Readers*

YOUNG COUSINS MYSTERIES
by Elspeth Campbell Murphy

Rib-tickling mysteries just for beginning readers—with Timothy, Titus, and Sarah-Jane from the THREE COUSINS DETECTIVE CLUB®.

WATCH OUT FOR JOEL!
by Sigmund Brouwer

Seven-year-old Joel is always getting into scrapes—despite his older brother, Ricky, always being told, "Watch out for Joel!"

Series for Young Readers†

ASTROKIDS™
by Robert Elmer

Space scooters? Floating robots? Jupiter ice cream? Blast into the future for out-of-this-world, zero-gravity fun with the AstroKids on space station *CLEO-7*.

THE CUL-DE-SAC KIDS
by Beverly Lewis

Each story in this lighthearted series features the hilarious antics and predicaments of nine endearing boys and girls who live on Blossom Hill Lane.

JANETTE OKE'S ANIMAL FRIENDS
by Janette Oke

Endearing creatures from the farm, forest, and zoo discover their place in God's world through various struggles, mishaps, and adventures.

THREE COUSINS DETECTIVE CLUB®
by Elspeth Campbell Murphy

Famous detective cousins Timothy, Titus, and Sarah-Jane learn compelling Scripture-based truths while finding—and solving—intriguing mysteries.

*(ages 6–8)   †(ages 7–10)

03B